THE GIANT'S EMBRACE

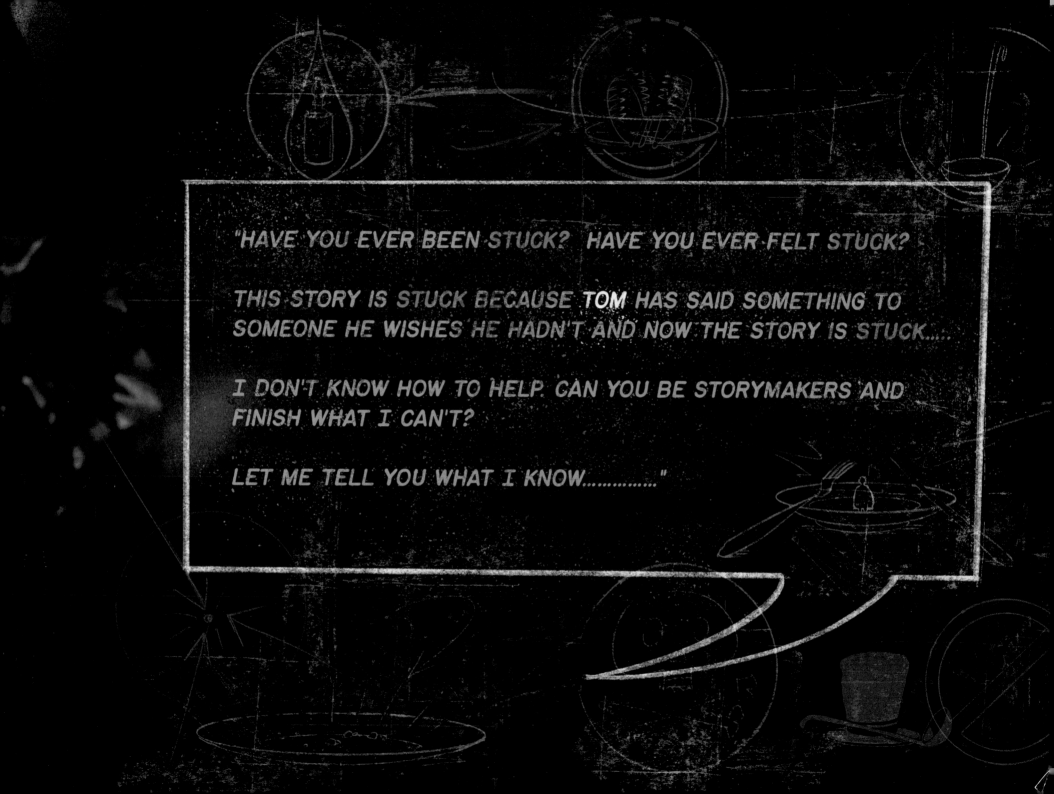

"HAVE YOU EVER BEEN STUCK? HAVE YOU EVER FELT STUCK?

THIS STORY IS STUCK BECAUSE TOM HAS SAID SOMETHING TO SOMEONE HE WISHES HE HADN'T AND NOW THE STORY IS STUCK......

I DON'T KNOW HOW TO HELP. CAN YOU BE STORYMAKERS AND FINISH WHAT I CAN'T?

LET ME TELL YOU WHAT I KNOW............."

ONCE THERE WAS A VERY, VERY, VERY GREEDY *GIANT*

THE GIANT WOULD SIT AND EAT AND EAT AND EAT UNTIL HE COULD EAT NO MORE.

IT WAS BECAUSE OF THE GIANT'S GREED THAT THE LITTLE PEOPLE WENT HUNGRY.

IT HAD NOT ALWAYS BEEN SO. THERE WAS A TIME WHEN HE USED TO BE A FRIEND AND A HELPER TO THE LITTLE PEOPLE, BUT NOW HE ONLY CARED ABOUT HIS *GREAT BIG BELLY.*

THE *GIANT* WOULD EAT EVERYTHING AND ANYTHING WHEN IT TOOK HIS FANCY, EVEN THE GRASS ON THE HILLS AND THE LEAVES ON THE TREES.

THE LITTLE PEOPLE COWERED WITH FEAR WHENEVER THEY HEARD THE GIANT'S FOOTSTEPS, AS HE ROAMED THE GREAT FOREST IN SEARCH OF HIS NEXT MEAL....

BOOM!
BOOM!
BOOM!

AT THE EDGE OF THE FOREST IN A TINY LITTLE HOVEL, *LIVED MOTHER AND HER TWO SONS.*
THE ELDEST SON, TOM, WAS A LIVELY LAD WHO WAS ALWAYS BEING MADE TO FETCH AND
CARRY FOR HIS BABY BROTHER WHO CRIED AND CRIED AND CRIED TO BE FED.

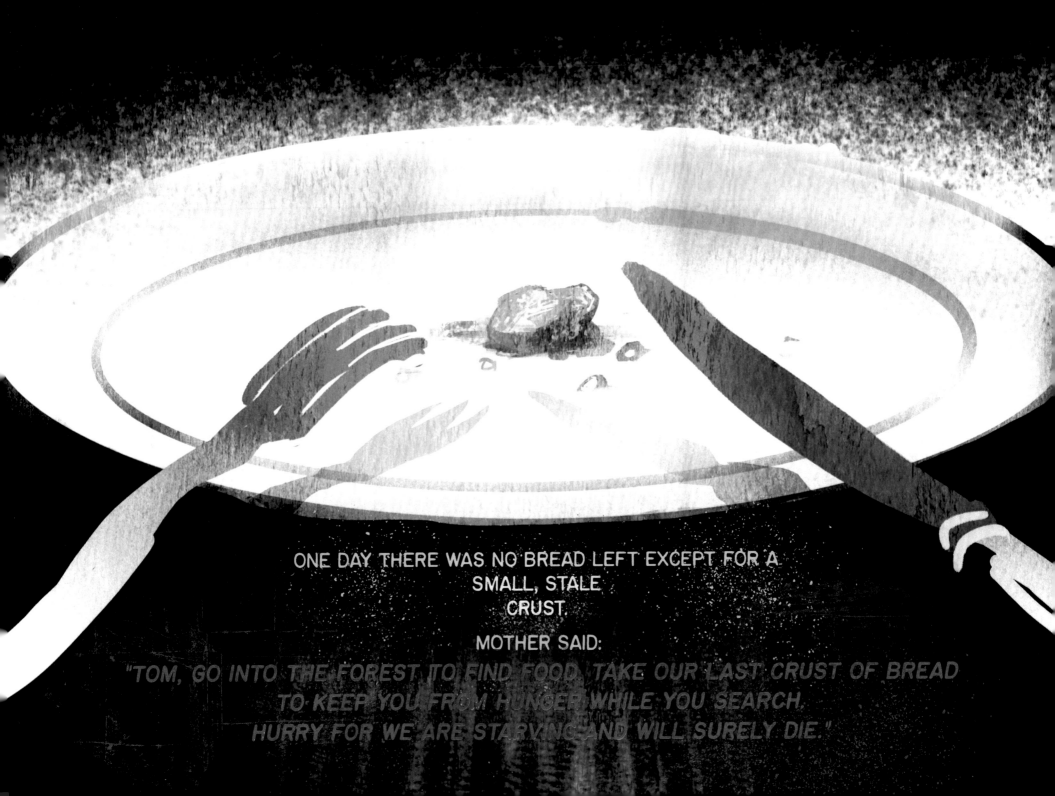

ONE DAY THERE WAS NO BREAD LEFT EXCEPT FOR A
SMALL, STALE
CRUST.

MOTHER SAID:

"TOM, GO INTO THE FOREST TO FIND FOOD. TAKE OUR LAST CRUST OF BREAD
TO KEEP YOU FROM HUNGER WHILE YOU SEARCH.
HURRY FOR WE ARE STARVING AND WILL SURELY DIE."

THE GREAT FOREST WAS A DARK, FRIGHTFUL PLACE.

THE ANIMALS CREPT AWAY TO HIDE AND THE BIRDS CEASED TO SING, A SAD HUSH HUNG OVER THE FOREST.

TOM BEGAN TO FEEL SO,   SO SMALL AND ALONE.

TO KEEP UP HIS STRENGTH IN HIS SEARCH, TOM DECIDED TO REST AND NIBBLE ON THE CRUST OF BREAD.

SUDDENLY, TOM WAS STARTLED TO HEAR A SORROWFUL SQUEAK.

SLUMPED ON A NEARBY TREE STUMP WAS A MOUSE, A LITTLE CREATURE WITH A HUGE HUNGER.

"PLEASE KIND SIR, SPARE ME A CRUMB OF YOUR CRUST."

TOM LOOKED AT THE CRUST AND BACK TO THE MOUSE AND BACK TO THE CRUST.............COULD HE?

TOM WAS NOT MADE OF STONE, SO HE FED THE STARVING CREATURE A CRUMB AND MORE UNTIL THE CRUST HAD GONE AND THE MOUSE WAS WELL AGAIN.

"YOUR KIND HEART I WILL NOT FORGET. WHEN YOU ARE IN NEED, MOUSE WILL HURRY TO YOUR SIDE."

AND THE

MOUSE

VANISHED

LEAVING TOM

ALONE ONCE MORE

ON WENT TOM, DEEPER AND DEEPER INTO THE VERY HEART OF THE FOREST.

BOOM! BOOM! BOOM!

HUNGRY TOM WAS AT THE POINT OF GIVING UP WHEN HE STUMBLED INTO A CLEARING.

THERE, FAST ASLEEP, LAY THE GIANT. TOM WANTED TO RUN BUT HE COULD SEE THAT

IN THE GIANT'S LADLE WAS SOME LEFTOVER FOOD.........

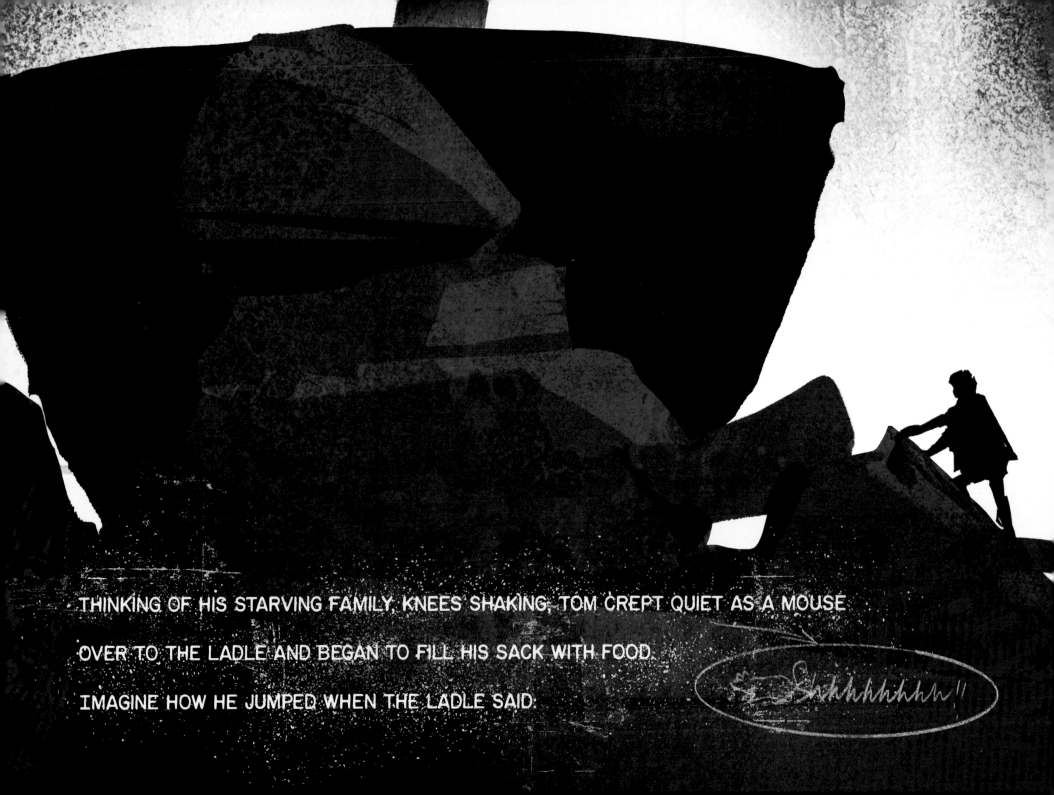

THINKING OF HIS STARVING FAMILY, KNEES SHAKING, TOM CREPT QUIET AS A MOUSE

OVER TO THE LADLE AND BEGAN TO FILL HIS SACK WITH FOOD.

IMAGINE HOW HE JUMPED WHEN THE LADLE SAID:

Shhhhhhh!!

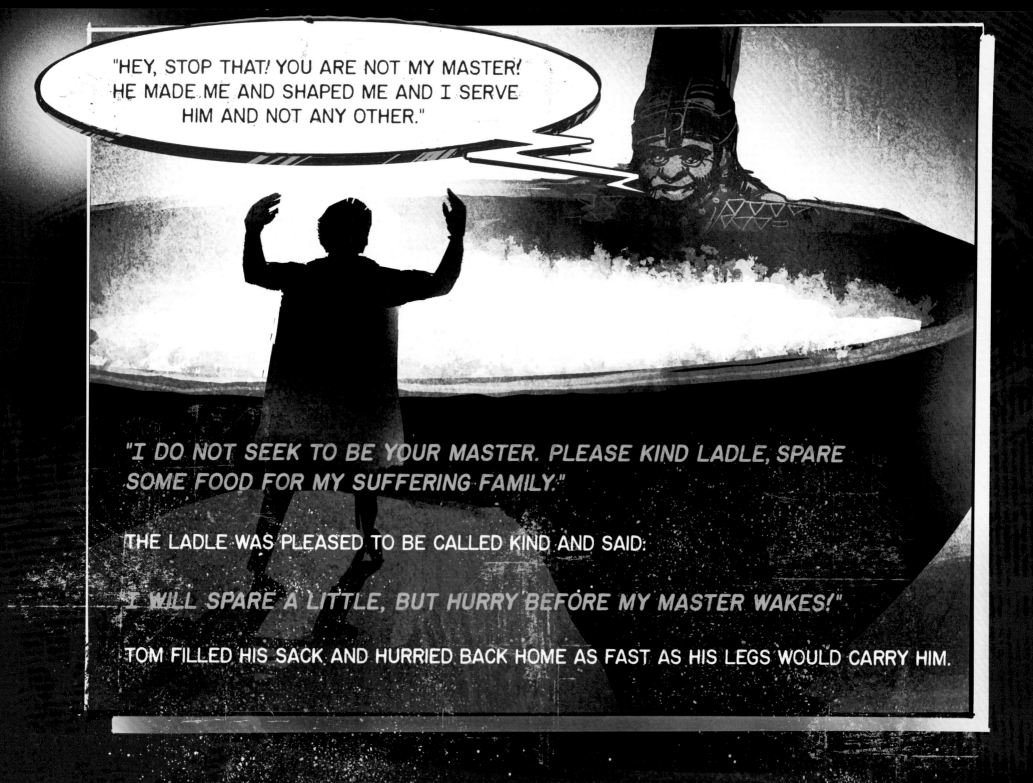

WHEN TOM GOT HOME, HIS MOTHER HUGGED HIM AND SAID,

"YOU BRAVE BOY, YOU CLEVER BOY, FOR YOU HAVE SAVED US!"

AND THEY FEASTED ON THE FOOD UNTIL THEY HAD ROOM FOR NO MORE.

BUT AS SUMMER TURNS TO WINTER, ALL GOOD THINGS COME TO AN END........

MOTHER SAID, "GO INTO THE FOREST. TAKE OUR LAST DROP OF WATER ON YOUR SEARCH. WE ARE THIRSTY AND WILL SURELY DIE."

'YES MOTHER, I WILL NOT RETURN UNTIL THE JOB IS DONE." REPLIED TOM......

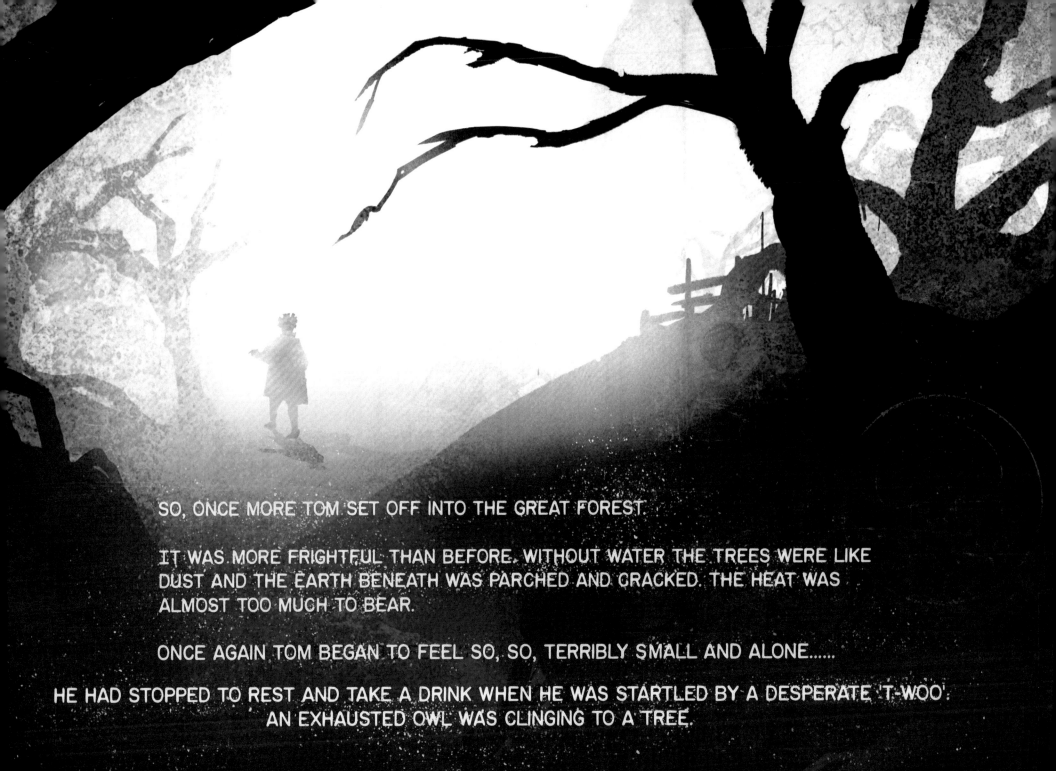

SO, ONCE MORE TOM SET OFF INTO THE GREAT FOREST.

IT WAS MORE FRIGHTFUL THAN BEFORE. WITHOUT WATER THE TREES WERE LIKE DUST AND THE EARTH BENEATH WAS PARCHED AND CRACKED. THE HEAT WAS ALMOST TOO MUCH TO BEAR.

ONCE AGAIN TOM BEGAN TO FEEL SO, SO, TERRIBLY SMALL AND ALONE......

HE HAD STOPPED TO REST AND TAKE A DRINK WHEN HE WAS STARTLED BY A DESPERATE 'T-WOO'. AN EXHAUSTED OWL WAS CLINGING TO A TREE.

"PLEASE, I BEG YOU TO SPARE A DROP OF WATER!"

TOM LOOKED AT THE FLASK AND BACK TO THE OWL, THEN BACK TO THE FLASK.......COULD HE?

TOM'S HEART WOULD NOT LET HIM STAND IDLY BY AND SEE THE POOR CREATURE DIE.
HE SPARED A DROP AND MORE UNTIL THERE WAS NO MORE WATER TO GIVE.

"T-WOO. I THANK YOU MY FRIEND - CALL UPON ME WHEN YOU ARE IN NEED.
OWL WILL COME, T-WOO."

BOOM! BOOM! BOOM!

BRAVE TOM STUMBLED ONCE MORE INTO THE CLEARING. THERE, AS BEFORE, THE GIANT LAY FAST ASLEEP, GRIPPING HIS LADLE. TOM COULD SEE WATER; PLENTY OF IT TO A LITTLE PERSON LIKE HIM, IT LAY LIKE A POND IN THE LADLE.

SO WITH SHAKING LEGS HE FLITTED, SILENT AS AN OWL, OVER TO THE LADLE AND BEGAN TO FILL HIS FLASK.

TOM HURRIED BACK AS FAST AS HIS LEGS WOULD CARRY HIM.........

HE KNEW THAT BEFORE LONG EVERYTHING
WOULD BE GONE......

MOTHER SAID,

"GO TO THE FOREST,
TAKE THIS KNIFE, WE ARE STARVING
AND THIRSTY,
WITHOUT YOUR HELP WE WILL SURELY
DIE......."

"YES MOTHER,"

REPLIED TOM.

TOM VENTURED ONCE MORE INTO THE DEATHLY FOREST.

IT HAD BECOME SUCH A MOURNFUL, PRICKLY, THICKETY PLACE.

TOM FELT THAT HORRIBLE FEELING OF BEING SO, SO SMALL: SMALLER THAN HE HAD EVER FELT BEFORE.

MANY HOURS LATER, TIRED AND HUNGRY AND THIRSTY TOM DECIDED TO REST.

IT WAS THEN THAT HE SAW A YOUNG DEER CAUGHT IN A TRAP.

DESPERATE TOM DREW HIS KNIFE WITH LUNCH ON HIS MIND BUT THE DEER
CALLED OUT TO HIM,

"PLEASE, PLEASE FREE ME FROM THIS TERRIBLE TRAP!"

TOM LOOKED AT THE KNIFE AND BACK TO THE DEER THEN BACK TO THE KNIFE.
HE COULD USE IT RIGHT NOW TO FEED AND SAVE HIS FAMILY.......SHOULDN'T HE?

BUT TOM COULD NOT BEAR TO SEE SUCH SUFFERING AND FREED HER.

"IF YOU STAND TO FALL I WILL RUSH LIKE THE WIND TO YOUR CALL!"

SHE SAID AND BOUNDED AWAY.

ON WENT UNBREAKABLE TOM INTO THE VERY HEART OF THE FOREST.......BACK
TO THE GIANT'S CLEARING.

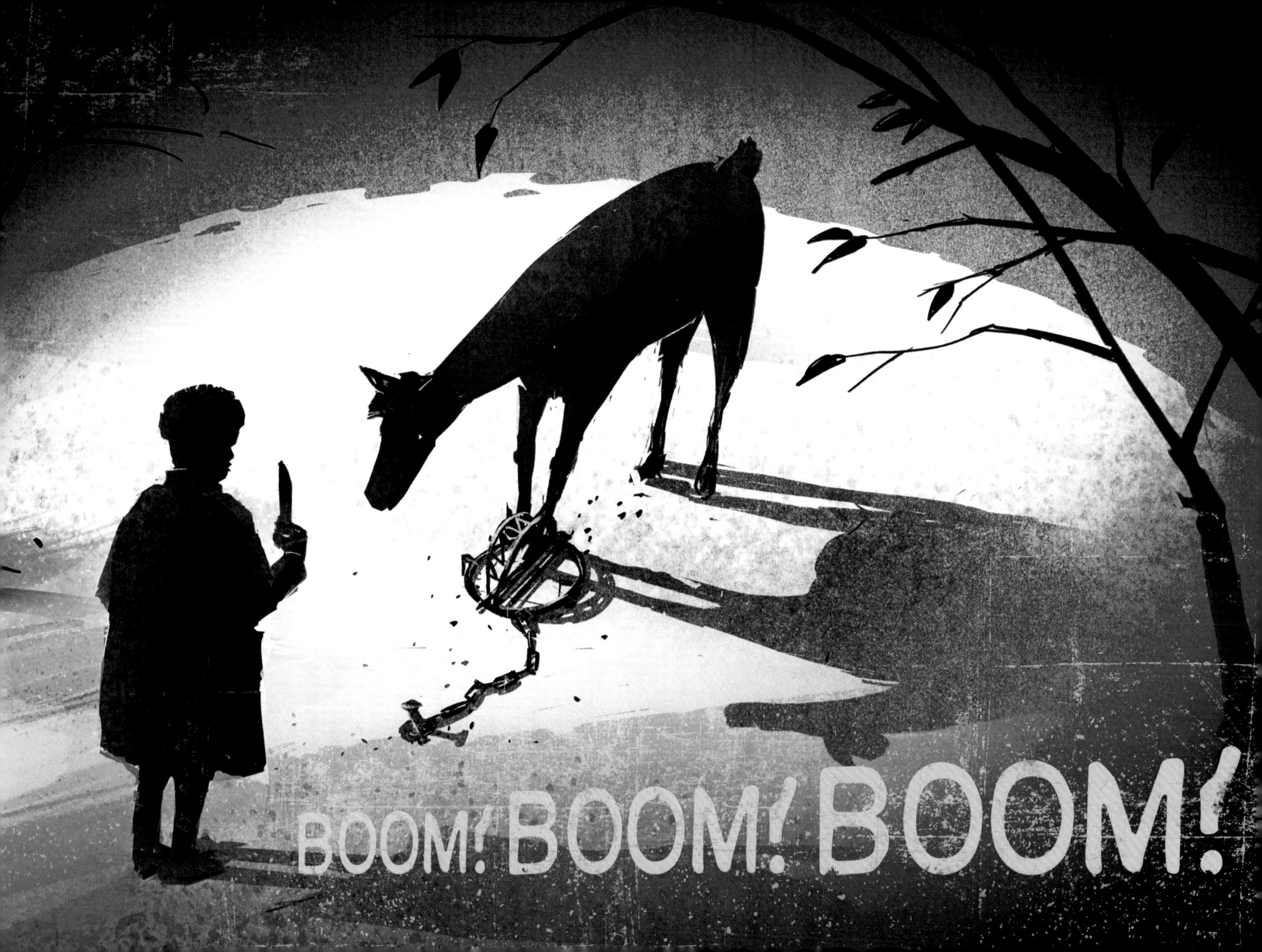
BOOM! BOOM! BOOM!

THE GIANT LAY SLEEPING WITH THE LADLE TIGHTLY GRIPPED IN HIS HAND.

WITH THE SPRING OF A DEER, TOM CLIMBED UP TO THE LADLE ONLY TO FIND TO HIS HORROR
THAT THERE WAS NOTHING INSIDE.

AND THE LADLE SAID,

*"HELP ME!! THE GIANT WILL EXPECT ME TO SERVE HIM WHEN HE WAKES
BUT THERE IS NOTHING LEFT TO FEED HIM!"*

TOM WAS NOT PREPARED FOR THIS. THE KNIFE DROPPED FROM HIS HAND AND LANDED
WITH A CLANG AND RING INSIDE THE EMPTY LADLE..........

TOM QUIVERED AS HE WAS LOCKED IN THE GIANT'S EMBRACE.

"WHAT THIEF COMES TO STEAL FROM THE GIANT?!!'

IT WAS THEN THAT THE GIANT HAD A NEW IDEA,

"GIANT WANTS DINNER. HMMMMM, GIANT WILL LIKE THE TASTE OF MAN FLESH!"

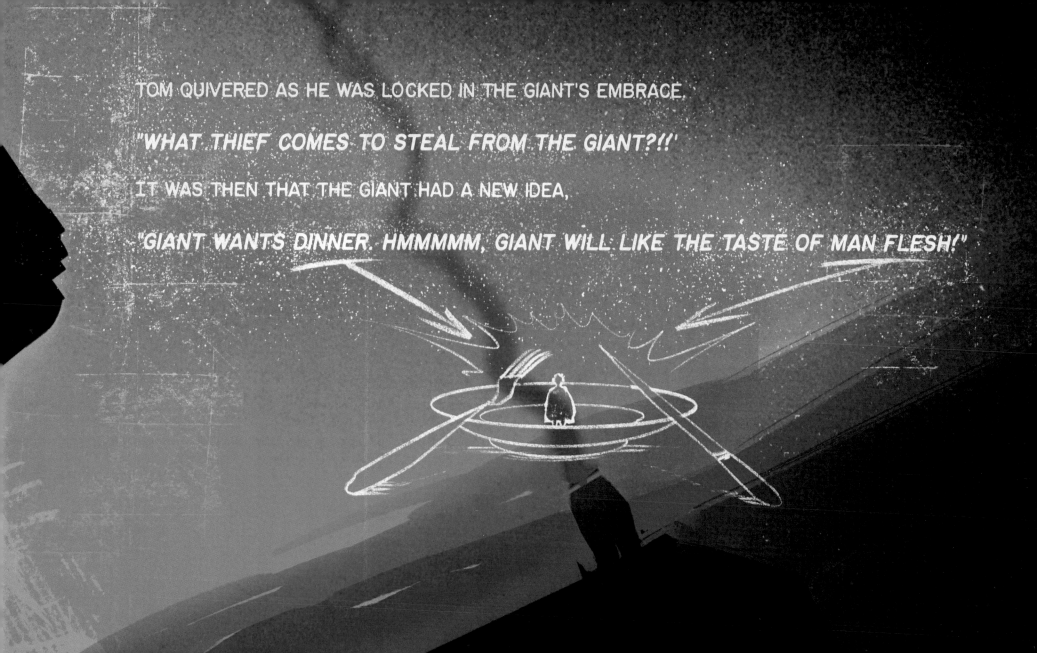

AFRAID TO DIE, YOUNG HOPELESS TOM OFFERED HIS MOTHER AND BABY BROTHER! THE GREEDY GIANT, WHO ALWAYS WANTED MORE, SPARED TOM HIS LIFE IN RETURN FOR THEM.

"BRING THEM HERE TOMORROW."
UNABLE TO RETURN HOME AND ASHAMED OF HIS PROMISE, TOM WANDERED AWAY.......

DEEP IN THE FOREST TOM BEGAN TO CRY. IN THE SHADOWS VIEWED THE MOUSE, WATCHED THE OWL AND PEEPED THE DEER. ALL WONDERING HOW TO EASE TOM'S ACHING HEART.

"YOU HEARD THE PROMISE THAT TOM MADE TO THE GIANT BUT IT CAN'T BE LEFT THERE......

CAN YOU HELP TOM?

CAN YOU SEE WHAT IS NEEDED TO FINISH THIS STORY?

I KNOW HIS OTHER FRIENDS, THE ANIMALS WANT TO HELP TOO BUT HOW CAN A TINY MOUSE, AN OWL AND A DEER HELP AGAINST A GIANT?

THEY ALL NEED YOUR IDEAS, YOUR THOUGHTS AND YOUR ADVICE

ONLY THEN WILL TOM KNOW WHAT TO DO.

The Giant's Embrace Resources

There are four sections to these resources:

1. Things to do before the story

2. Things to do after the story

3. Things to think about

4. Resources

The following teaching ideas and resources aim to support teachers in a programme of work, based on this book and the digital version of 'The Giant's Embrace'. Each activity can work independently, as well as part of the whole programme of work and is aimed at learners in the EYFS and in Key Stage 1. However, the activities are aimed at 'stages, not ages' so wherever appropriate, each activity is accompanied by adaptations to 'step up' or 'step down' to meet the needs of all learners.

These ideas could also be used by parents or carers. They are in no way exhaustive but offer a starting point which we are sure you will add to, develop, and change to suit your children.

This material is also supported by further online resources for teachers and parents.

We have placed a giant hat with a number in the corner of pages that correlate with the tasks below. More ideas can be found on our website.

1. Things to do before the story

Question to begin the exploration

Ask the child/children:

I was wondering what stories you know?

Do you know any 'Once upon a time …' stories?

We think that drawing on the classic stories will be very beneficial (which is not to say that hearing about modern stories will not be). Giving space to what they know and are familiar with, democratises the space: we are not placing value judgement on their stories or even which stories they do or do not know. We are creating a 'crucible' - a space full of us and our stories.

Ask:

What is your favourite part of the story?

Do you all know that story?

For example, Hansel and Gretel:

'That must have been a difficult decision for the parents to make …'

'They must have been starving.'

'When the parents came home and heard nothing but silence, how did they stop themselves going back to get the children?'

Looking ahead to the last task - helping Tom to help himself

The stories that emerge in this initial exploration might be useful at the end when trying to finish the story of 'The Giant's Embrace', for example the clever solution Hansel and particularly Gretel use in freeing themselves.

Ask:

Have you ever been stuck?

Have you ever felt stuck?

Tom has said something he wishes he had not said.

Ask: Have you ever said something you wish you had not said?

Take the children's responses …

who did you say it to?

how did it make them feel?

how did it make you feel?

The story

It is time to hear the story … are you ready? Let us begin.

2. Things to do after the story

Request from the story

Explain:

You heard the promise Tom made to the Giant, but it can't be left there …

Can you help Tom? Can you see what is needed to finish this story?

I know his other friends, the animals, want to help too … but how can a tiny mouse, an owl and deer help against a giant?

They all need your ideas, your thoughts and your advice. Only then will Tom know what to do.

Only then will Tom's family be saved, and the story will be unstuck at last.

Task 1

Discuss the promise with the children

Ask:

Did you hear the promise?

Would you have made such a promise?

I wonder why he did it, then?

How do you think he feels?

What would his mother/the animals /the ladle say to him about what he promised?

What would you say to Tom about what he promised?

Task 2

Explain:

But it cannot be left there ... Can you help Tom?

Now that the child/children have reflected on Tom's state of being and have discussed their opinion on the promise, we can begin to help.

Like all good stories, this one needs a resolution. The resolution is always present within the constraints of the story. These internal constraints evoke the imagination, and the children can seek solutions which adhere to the story's internal logic.

Stepping out of the story's logic moves the child away from imaginative solutions and into fantasy. However, children cannot utilise magic in their world to solve the dilemmas they encounter. In fantasy, the mouse could wield magic or be indestructible, but within the logic of *'The Giant's Embrace'*, the mouse isn't either of these things: if she had been, she would not have been half-starved.

However, the mouse does possess skills that come with being small, and these attributes lead themselves to dealing with a Giant. For example, she could, undetected, crawl into the Giant's ear and shout.

Invite the children to come up with a plan to help Tom out of his situation. The plan should include the animals, the forest, the objects in the story, even Tom's Mother and baby brother. Unfortunately, the children can't offer physical help as they are not in the story, although they could act out any solution to validate the plan.

Story Mountain

Teaching Input	The storyteller, Kate, says *'the stories you know have a beginning, a middle and an end.'* Ask the children to think about stories that they know well and to consider their beginning, middle and end. Model to the children how to complete a story mountain for a story that is familiar to them (see Resource 1).
Individual/Group Activity	Encourage children to complete a story mountain, using images or words, for a given story.
Step Up	Children could complete a story mountain for a story of their own devising. Children could use their completed story mountain as a planning tool for an extended piece of writing.
Step Down	Give children images from a story that is familiar to them and ask them to place them in the appropriate places on the story mountain.
Bring it Together	Children share examples of their story mountain for familiar tales. Can their friends identify the story from its mountain?

Language development

Binary Opposites

These are the most basic and powerful tools for organising and categorising knowledge. We see such opposites in conflict in nearly all stories, and they are crucial in providing an initial ordering to many complex forms of knowledge. The most powerfully engaging opposites - like good/bad, security/fear, competition/cooperation - are emotionally charged and, when attached to content, imaginatively engaging.

Binary Opposites

- Emotionally charged.

- Children are already experts.

- Are how we learn to understand our world.

- We can understand something we already know further by exploring its opposite.

- A way of testing.

- They are fixed truths - culture changes and defines concepts in new ways; we find our values in relation to them.

- Two extremes to measure ourselves in relation with.

Related to metaphor and being in the metaphors; the binary opposites are active, they (children) test their abilities - trapped (can escape on the horse), slow (the horse offers speed), power, hunger etc.

Children are constantly in a state of passing through/crossing thresholds, from known to unknown. The process of learning and growing and living is one of moving between binary opposites, negating one into/through another. Tom's journey is the same.

There are many binaries consciously built into the story: full and empty, big and small, brave and scared. However, there are others that can be found in the story. One that jumps to mind comes from the description of the hovel. You could explore the concept of Home, perhaps asking what the difference is between house and home … … what is Tom's hovel, is it a house or home? The exploration with the young people can become exciting, as sometimes both experiences can exist at the same time: sometimes it's home; other times, house. Tom's experience must be the same sensation all young people feel.

Rhyme, Rhythm, and Pattern

These are potent tools for giving meaningful, memorable and attractive shape to any content. Their roles in learning are numerous, and their power to engage the imagination in learning the rhythms and patterns of language - and the underlying emotions that they reflect - is enormous. They are important in learning all symbol systems, like mathematics and music, and all forms of knowledge and experience.

Rhyme, Rhythm, and Pattern

- Help children to remember things.

- Parts of how we learn and interpret as humans - we already have these capacities.

- Pattern embeds ideas.

- Rhyme and rhythm pervade our language and lives.

- Meaningful, memorable, and attractive – give shape to content.

Look for the patterns, the rhymes and the rhythm in the story. Encourage the children to match them in their own written work.

Metaphor

This is the tool that enables us to see one thing in terms of another. This peculiar ability lies at the heart of human intellectual inventiveness, creativity and imagination. It is important to help students keep this ability vividly alive by exercising it frequently. Using it frequently in teaching will help students learn to read with energy and flexibility.

Metaphor

- Makes connections.
- Seeing one thing in terms of another.
- Helps shape understanding through its poetry.

Look for the metaphors. Once found, see if they can be deepened.

Question:

Can you be hungry for more than food ?

Can you be hungry for love?

I wonder what else he has been starved of?

Have you ever been fed up?

Felt fed up?

The Giant

Teaching Input	We learnt that before the story started the Giant was a 'friend and helper to the little people'. Ask the children what things the villagers might have needed help with, that the Giant would be good at doing e.g. building a bridge.
	Consider why the Giant stopped being a friend and began to destroy and eat everything in his path? Encourage the children to think about different points in the Giant's life, in order to understand the change e.g. the first time that the Giant got into trouble for something that he did not do, or the first time he was left out of a game.
Individual/Group Activity	Use the outline of the Giant (Resource 2) and label around the outside of the Giant with adjectives to describe what he looks like. Inside the outline, add adjectives to describe how he feels and thinks.
Step Up	Write a passage, from the Giant's perspective, describing how and why he stopped being a 'friend and helper to the little people'.
Step Down	Complete the Group Activity, with an adult to act as scribe. Take the opportunity to extend and enrich children's vocabulary e.g. "He's definitely ugly, I agree. I know another word that means 'ugly' – can I add 'hideous?'"

Bring it Together   After feeding back ideas on ways to describe the Giant, ask an adult, or a child who is confident to do so, to be in role as the Giant. Encourage others to ask the Giant about his thoughts and feelings, including why he changed towards the little people.

Comparing Giants

Teaching Input   Ask the children about any other stories they know, which have giants as characters, establishing that they are a popular character in traditional tales but that their portrayal may be different in each story.

Share with them, the story of 'The Selfish Giant' by Oscar Wilde.

Individual/Group Activity   Children discuss ways in which the Giant from Tom's story is the same as The Selfish Giant and ways in which he is different. Ideas can be recorded on large pieces of sugar paper for sharing with the larger group, later.

Step Up   Children could independently complete the written chart (Resource 3).

Step Down   Choose a text more suitable for these learners e.g. 'The Giant of Yum' by Elli Wollard, or 'The Smartest Giant in Town' by Julia Donaldson.

Bring it Together   Invite children to share their ideas about the similarities and differences between the characters they have been considering.

Exploring the Giant's Dreams

Teaching Input   We heard that after all the food is gone, the forest is bare and the Giant sucks his thumb, still gripping the ladle. Encourage the children to consider what the Giant might dream of, sharing their thoughts and ideas with each other.

Individual/Group Activity   Provide the children with a variety of materials e.g. paint, pastels, collaging materials and ask them to create an image that might come directly from the Giant's dream.

Step Up   Complete the same creative activity but consider what Tom might be dreaming of. This might be different at different points in his journey e.g. before he had ever seen the Giant; after he had stolen from the Giant and after he had overcome the Giant.

Bring it Together   Give children the opportunity to explain their choices of materials and effects, as well as the content of the image they have created. Encourage them to relate their image to previous work on their exploration of the Giant's character.

After the Story (version a)

Teaching Input	Explain that now the Giant has been defeated, the village needs to decide on the best way of avoiding anything like this happening again.
Individual/Group Activity	Children could come up with a set of village rules to be followed, in order to ensure that the little people remain safe.
Step Up	Put the children in role as the villagers themselves, thinking about what they need to think about and do.
Step Down	Offer an oral sentence structure to support children in offering their ideas e.g. "The little people need to…"
Bring it Together	Decide on a way to display these rules, along with any other work done on 'The Giant's Embrace'.

After the Story (version b)

Teaching Input	Explain that now the Giant has been defeated, the village needs to decide on the best way of avoiding anything like this happening again.
Individual/Group Activity	Tell the children that they are going to plant a 'story tree' that will grow in the village and bear the stories that the villagers must never forget. Ask each child to contribute a 'leaf' (see Resource 4) to the story tree, allowing them the choice of how to best represent the story.
Bring it Together	Create a story tree display, to showcase the children's ideas, along with any other work done on "The Giant's Embrace".

3. Things to think about

The following comes from Big Brum's practice, but we think it may be useful to you as a teacher or other adult when developing ideas from the story with children.

The angle of connection

This is about giving space to an individual child to relate their personal experience to a moment of the story that they know and like. It then involves taking these moments and finding a unifying or shared experience for the class (social), while linking it to our story (centre)

The centre in 'The Giants Embrace'

All stories have a centre or central question. The centre of a story is different from a moral. One way of saying this is that the centre deals with justice, whereas morals concentrate on injustice. The centre gives children space for exploration and discovery: it does not transmit or tell them how to live but opens space for them to think about how we are living. Morals instruct us or tell us how to live.

In 'The Giant's Embrace', the central question for Big Brum is:

How do we live humanly when we cannot hear the cries of the hungry over the Giant's stamping feet?

The cry

There are children literally crying in the story. Tom's baby brother continues to cry throughout the story. We know that he is hungry, the greedy Giant is eating everything, and the little people are starving. Perhaps the cries also express that the little people, who are forced into living just to survive, are being starved of more than food? How are the other characters 'crying'? What else might they have been starved of or perhaps fed up with?

So, in all the tasks that we offer when exploring the story of 'The Giants Embrace', one is listening for how the centre is expressing itself in the children who are hearing the story. This can begin by tuning one's ear to how 'the cry' is articulated in their favourite bits of other stories as well as in all the tasks and that follow. These are by no means exhaustive.

4. Copiable resources

These are also available as printable downloads.

Resource 1: Story Mountain

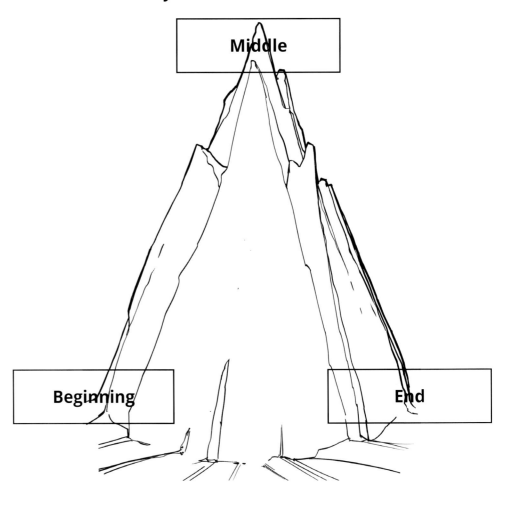

Resource 2: Giant outline

Resource 3: Comparing Giants

The Giant from "Giant's Embrace"	The Giant from_____

Resource 4. Story tree leaf

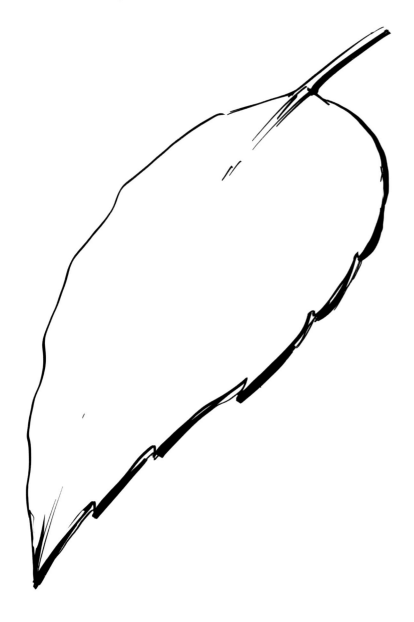